John Cameron Grant

Bits of Brazil

The legend of Lilith and other poems

John Cameron Grant

Bits of Brazil
The legend of Lilith and other poems

ISBN/EAN: 9783337391362

Printed in Europe, USA, Canada, Australia, Japan

Cover: Foto ©Andreas Hilbeck / pixelio.de

More available books at **www.hansebooks.com**

BITS OF BRAZIL,

THE LEGEND OF LILITH,

AND OTHER POEMS.

BY

JOHN CAMERON GRANT.

(AUTHOR OF "SONGS FROM THE SUNNY SOUTH;" "A YEAR OF LIFE;"
"PRAIRIE PICTURES;" ETC.)

LONDON:

LONGMANS, GREEN, AND CO.

1885.

TO

THOMAS, LORD WALSINGHAM,

THIS VOLUME

IN SLIGHT TOKEN OF AFFECTION AND ESTEEM.

———

" And Nature, the old nurse, took
The child upon her knee."

PREFACE.

DEAR LORD WALSINGHAM,—As you were chiefly instrumental in my making a voyage to this beautiful country, I have dedicated my little Volume to you. You are intimately acquainted with a great part of the Western and North-western States and Provinces of America, and were kind enough both to appreciate and to bear witness to the faithfulness to nature of my "Prairie Pictures," I now trust that you will find these slight sketches of the South equally true should you carry out your intended trip to Brazil.

IN THE BRAZILS,
1884.

INDEX.

BITS OF BRAZIL:—   PAGE.

    DOWN THE RIVER 1

    SUNSET STILL II

    THE LONG LAGOON 15

    PALMS AND PARTING DAY 20

    STORM STAID 23

    PIGMY PAMPAS 29

    A SHORE SCENE 35

THE LEGEND OF LILITH 41

FOR "T. C." 59

DIVINE DEATH 60

SOMEONE—I. 61

ADSUM—II. 62

PLIGHTED—III. 63

FOR A TRIPTYCH, BY HERBERT SCHMALZ 65

    THE STILL SILENT PAST 65

    THE DIM MVSTIC FUTURE 66

    THE PRESENT BITTER-SWEET 66

    FINAL 67

THE OAK ROOM, OXBOROUGH 68

IN MEMORIAM . . . . *Henry Fawcett* 72

IN MEMORIAM . . . *For Three Dead* 73

ENGLAND 1885 74

BITS OF BRAZIL.

DOWN THE RIVER.

I.

DENSE to the water's edge
    Dark forest, overhanging the dark rocks
        That hide below in denser growths and green
Of Canes and Reeds ; and set on every ledge
    Broad-leaved Bananas, whose reflection mocks
        The lazy Lotos on the wave beneath,
        Save where some surly Screw-pine comes between
        With cruel spines like some old Dragon's teeth.

II.

Floating upon the stream,
    A mass of leaves, the buoyant Water-plants,
        Crowned with pale lilac lilies on every stem,
Spread out their feathery roots and languid seem
    To swim where'er the creeping current slants.—
        There, like a ribbon shaken by the tide,
        And decked about with many a glittering gem,
        A Water-snake makes for the other side.

B

III.

Mimosa plants in flower
  Upon the bank, and dripping with a dew
    Of diamond flashed from every leaf you see,
For in three minutes came a tropic shower
  From one small cloud that stained the speckless blue
    And left these crystals ; tho this river-bed
    Is famed for diamonds, fairer far to me
      Are those bright diamonds glittering over head.

IV.

My Indian forest trees
  Are larger far than those we see around
    But these woods seem of thicker undergrowth,
And in a thousand strange varieties
  Is every bough with wondrous Orchids crowned,
    Some large, some small, of every shape and size,
    That cling with sinewy fingers like the Sloth
      That, Orchid-like, hangs there before our eyes.

V.

And every now and then
  A Skipping-fish goes flip, flip, o'er the wave
    With but three jumps however hard he strives.—
Two Lizards, lazy little gentlemen,
  Bask on the rocks, and, as you near the cave
    Made by the overhanging brow, the Prawn
    That sat beside them, like a great Frog dives
      Into the water leaving them forlorn.

VI.

There are two forests here,
  One in the water neath yon one in the air,
    The thick Lentana mingles where they meet
Along the bank line, full of Birds that clear
  Its branches of their berries, dainty fare,
      Scorned by the Humming Bird that poises light
    Neath that great flower-bell, just a sapphire fleet
    Gifted with wings and sent abroad for flight.

VII.

And on that tree hard by
  Two large black Birds, with great high shoulders set
    Above their snakey necks and thin long bills
And tiny heads—don't know their family :—
  There flash three scarlet Oriels that have met
      For morning converse :—there our Mocking Bird,
    That learns whatever word his master wills,
    Practising over some strange note he heard.

VIII.

In all the trees o'er head
  Great White-Ants' Nests, on which in rusty brown
    Some insect eating Birds are breakfasting,
But leave the Hornets' nests unbreakfasted
  Whose Sentries watch the gate of each rough town,—
      'Tis scarce a week ago when, as we went
    Along a river bank, we fell their sting
    Who roused a nest, be sure by accident.

IX.

Uprooted down the tide
   Floats a great tree, and a great Butterfly
     Poises and floats and wheels about its boughs :—
I'm sure the fish would take a fly if tried,
   For one rose at him as he dipped hard by.—
      The vegetation on the bank grows past
     Description, with its Butterflies that house
     On every flower or troop and circle fast.

X.

Now the wild Plantain trees
   With queer red flowers give place, and, Man's first
     friends
   Among the trees, their Cousins take it up,
For we have reached a clearing. By degrees
   Won, but scarce held, where lavish Nature spends
      Her wealth so much at random :—leave it thus
     Just for a week and with its great pink cup
     The ground is captured by Convolvulus.

XI.

But working Man is there,
   And there his palm-roofed house, o'er shadowed by
     Papaw, and Jack, and Mango, and a small
Sparse Banian with its rootlets in the air,
   And Piassava Palms that stand and sigh
      As the breeze touches them, and Coacoa Nuts,
     And palm-oil Palms, and, loveliest of them all,
     The Queen Areca the far sky-line cuts.

XII.

So our Canoe slips on,—
.It's just a great long log and hollowed out,
  And hard enough to write in, 'tis so crank,
With its two Paddle-men that stand upon
  The bow and stern and smoke and talk and shout
      To neighbouring craft ;—no wonder in the grass
    That Bull looks up and gazes from the bank
    Surprised indeed to see us safely pass.

XIII.

For we are loaded full
  And carrying down provisions for a Friend,
    Down to the little Town upon the sea
At the stream's mouth, for there the Church doth rule
  To-morrow's *Festa;* without stint or end
      Of squibs and crackers honouring St. John's Day ;
    And we bring aids to the festivity
    Of all the up-country produce that we may.

XIV.

Here we are stopped to rest—
  A Hunter meets us with his promised game
    Neatly done up in green leaves, praying us
Excuse the quantity :—his hunt had zest
  Enough for any Hunter, for the same
      Had cost him nigh his life and half his prey,
    For Forest Indians found and chased him thus,
    A running fight that lasted half the day.

XV.

There is not much romance
About a blow-pipe and a poisoned dart.—
The Prairie Indian is all well enough,
And I've known what it is to look askance
O'er every ridge and ready for the start,
But take instead a dense dark forest round
Where all you'll hear may be's a little puff,
Feel a slight prick and know your mortal wound.

XVI.

But we must on again —
Look,—some dead Beast upon that sand bank there,
Two Vultures on it at their beastly meal.—
They're frightened, yes, but still you fired in vain.
To shoot with a revolver taxes fair
The best of shots, and you must practise till
All thought of sight or aim is nought, you feel
You've but to see the thing and you can kill.

XVII.

As we get further down
The huts become more frequent, and the small
Canoes keep passing, each one singly manned,
Full of Farinha, Cane, and Jerked-beef brown,
Dried Codfish, Beans, and earthern Pitchers tall,
Some carrying fish up from the stake nets, some
Drawn up to wait their owners on the sand
Like sleeping Alligators still and dumb.

XVIII.

Growing along the bank
  Wild Guava trees till you just loathe sight
    Of the green and yellow fruit, and here a patch
Of Coffee or of Cocoa, wild and rank
  But bent on bearing fruit with all their might
      Spite of the scant attention :—certainly
    This is a wondrous Land that none can match
      Where Man holds nature without toil in fee

XIX.

Here is the Sugar Mill
  Where we stop for our lazy mid-day meal,—
    The Mistress lazy, kindly, indolent,
The troop of Slaves that come and go at will,
  Slavery in one sense here they do not feel
      And, tho' the thought is hateful, I believe
    That better often thus their lives are spent
      Than in the freedom that they may receive.

XX.

For they're a kindly Race
  The true Brazilians, and in many ways
    Like our old Highland folk; most dignified,
Courteous, and hospitable, in their place
  Ruling their own, and humble all their days
      To Father and to Mother :—I of course
    Speak not of those that Towns have turned aside
      And touched with vice and foreign intercourse.

XXI.

Again we're off, behind
  Rise the blue Hills, those dark blue Hills I love
    Always to see about me where I go,
That bring up thoughts of India on the mind,
  And thoughts of Scotland, and of many a cove
    Along the shores of Italy, and bring
      The Foot-hill Prairies back, and then the Snow
        On those high Hills that know the eagle's wing.

XXII.

The river grows more wide
  And now and then a splendid isle divides
    The stream in two, clothed to the wave in green,
And we are in the influence of the tide.
  The wild Swamp-cotton grows along the sides
    With red and yellow flowers, and here and there
      A patch of Cane or Reed breaks on the scene
        With long spears trembling tufted in the air.

XXIII.

And nearer to the Sea
  The broad black banks of rich and slimy slush
    With twenty thousand tangled Mangrove roots
Crab-haunted,—hateful as they seem to me :—
  Ghoul-like they crouch and batten 'twixt the rush
    Of tide and tide, and like the Polyps grow
      That clutched all things with ever spreading shoots
        I read of in a Sea-tale long ago.

XXIV.

Here, as we slowly pass,
　Crabs climb most calmly into the Canoe ;—
　　I never knew it done in other Lands,
Without so much as by your leave, mere farce
　To ask :—they just did all they wished to do,
　　　Foraging round, and without fear or shame
　　Using their nippers like a pair of hands
　　And taking first of whatsoever came.

XXV.

Now evening comes apace
　With distant bells that ring their even-song,
　　Cease, and then chatter out like noisy Jays.—
For everyone holds *Festa* in the Place,
　And without bells no feast could get along,
　　　Where all the morning Men were piling ricks
　　Of logs and brushwood ; wont there be a blaze
　　To-night of fireworks and crackling sticks !

XXVI.

There, o'er the low hill's brow,
　You see the noisy gabled belfry tower
　　Beyond the little Town, our present port.—
A few stray goats, a pig and wandering cow
　Beginning to feed homewards at this hour,
　　　Some timber, rough hewn, waiting for the tide ;—
　　The long stake net, and, with the fish he's caught,
　　The Fisher paddling to the other side.

XXVII.

A Cape turned brings in view
  The line of Cocoanuts risen on the right
    That rises with the roaring of the sea
That shows its white teeth on the Bar, and thro
  The white foam show the rocks as black as night,
      Until the thundrous surge swells up again,
      Again to fall, where ever ceaselessly
          Upon the bright sand breaks the Atlantic Main !

SUNSET STILL.

———•◦•———

I.

THE sea is stilled in the silence, the sound of the voice
    of the sea
  Has lost its sorrow and sadness and speaks in an
    undertone
To the great green world above her that looks down
    lovingly,
  Nor bears in her mind the surges that raved on her
    ribs of stone.

II.

For silent in adoration the Earth takes leave of the Sun
  Like some old Aztec King from his Pyramid heights of
    power,
When all his People prayed and a thousand heads like
    one
  Were bowed to the god of glory that passed with the
    evening hour.

III.

Here never a sound or whisper while earth and sea and
  skies
  Were silent a space together like some lone central
  star,
In the holy calm of sunset that dies when the daylight
  dies
  And the night draws up in darkness from the Dreamland Isles afar.—

IV.

The Orange blossom is sweet but no Moth hovers
  above,
  Not even a Bat flits out and passes you like a
  ghost,
The very Birds are quiet, and never a tale of love
  Is shrilled or piped or whistled from the myriad insect
  host.

V.

The Palms seem all at prayer, and the Yucca's pointed
  leaves
  Like hands stretched up to Heaven, no Fern fronds
  bend and kiss.
And the great white-belled Datura wlth head bowed down
  receives
  The parting benediction in a beautiful dream of bliss.

VI.

No Ant is at work, already are stored the wondrous
    loads
  With which throughout the day their workers laboured
    so,
Marshalled like an army along their wonderful roads :—
  In the stillness one can almost hear the Creepers
    grow ! —

VII.

But there above like a ruddy gem on the Scorpion's
    back
  Antares gleams and glows, and the fires of Argo
    toss,
And low in the gulfs of space that the feet of the Centaur
    track
  Set for a symbol of hope the sign of the Southern
    Cross.

VIII.

And with the stars comes Night, and straight upon our
    ears
  The myriad tongues she hath take up the song of the
    night,
And the Owl swoops out like a shadow, and the Bat like
    a sailor steers
  Among the spikes of Cactus with swift unerring flight.

IX.

And the Forager-ants turn out, and the Night Hawk flies
     abroad,
   And the Snake is seeking its food, and the Cricket is
     mad with mirth,
And the toiling Spider builds or swings from his sticky
     cord,
   And the Hawk Moths rival the Humming Birds of the
     sunlit earth.

X.

And a voice comes from the forest, and over and far away
   Another voice makes answer from out the depths of the
     hill,
As Darkness calls her creatures to toil till the dawn of
     day
   For the spell of quiet is broken and passed is the Sun-
     set Still.

THE LONG LAGOON.

I

THE Palma Christi grows
  Along the shore thro thick Lentana brakes,
    And o'er them both the Piassava flings
Its ferny fronds into the air, and shows
  The blue sky thro its fingers the breeze shakes
    As if afraid of something lower down
    Where to its stem that snakey Orchid clings :—
    Beyond the Queen Areca's feathery crown !

II.

Here broad-leafed Plantain trees
  Bent neath their fruit, and lordly Cocoanut Palms,
    Bread-fruit, and Jack, and dark-leaved Mangoes
      rise ;—
Stretches of Sugar-cane, and mixed with these
  Roselles, Arnottoes, redolent of balms
    Some nameless plants, and creepers tangled thus
    A hundred ways, and jewelled Butterflies
    Courting the moony white Convolvulus.

III.

God-feeding Cacao plants,
   Sweet Limes, and Oranges, and Soursops,
     Great Sapotees, and fruitful Passion-vines,
And Palm-oil Palms, where, in the Sunlight slants,
   Basks the bright Lizard, shaded by wild Hops
      When the wind blows and makes their shadow
      dance
     Across him and that Dragon-fly that shines
      Like the bright steel-point of some warrior's lance.

IV.

An opening further on,
   And there the Hut with palm-leafed roof and shade
     Of forest trees about it, Caoutchouc,
Rose-wood, and that tree famed in Lebanon,
   And just in front a tiny grassy glade
      With three canoes drawn up and high and dry,—
     Two shadows following one another thro
      The light and shade from Kites that circle high.

V.

A flight of Parroquets
   Passing o'er head and chattering in their flight,
     They're settled down but ceaseless still in talk
And seemingly divided into sets
   For better converse ;—there 'll be rain to-night,—
      Those thee hoarse notes from out the forest tell
     Better than a Barometer :—that Hawk
      I'm glad to see those small Birds thrashing well.

VI.

We're in the Mangroves now
  Who sulk and watch for the returning tide,
    Dipping their dirty fingers in the mud,—
Like Children dabbling by some pier's dark slough—
  To hold them, when the stream has passed outside,
      Up full of Oysters, and with here and there,
    With white specked shell and nippers red as blood,
    A Crab that swings serenely in the air.

VII.

That thick brown mud and slime
  The young trees stand on in their long top boots,
    Stretching their arms to get them down as well,
And o'er them both the nimble brown Crabs climb
  Or sit like Squirrels perched upon the roots ;—
      Beneath the sickly waters run asea
    From desolation just made visible,
      As if they feared some awful thing might be

VIII.

Hidden in the drear world
  That none explore, the very crabs themselves
    Seem to keep to its borders : now and then
A water Snake, with all its length uncurled,
  Slips from your sight, and in the bottom delves
      And stirs the mud and all his lair surrounds
     And shrouds from view ; and, yet unknown to men,
    The silence breaks in melancholy sounds.

C

IX.

I hate the Mangrove swamps,
   Their fallen Oysters lying on the slush
     And the Crabs climbing over them, and great
Big Crabs more shy and fierce, and busy camps
   Of Soldier-Crabs :—just raise your hand,—a rush
      And each is in his house and then peeps out—
    That Robber-Crab, the nut drawn to his gate,
     Leaves it and bolts on seeing you about.

X.

A mass of roots no more,
   But Oysters, Crabs, and slime : I'm glad we've past
    The point and opened out another bay,
With grassy banks whereby in many a score
   Stand the white Cranes, that quick as lightning cast
     Their javelin beaks at any passing fish
    Albeit they look so solemn, and their prey
    At eve all told makes a fair Hunter's dish.

XI.

Now forest once again
   Down to the waters' edge, and then a break
    In the thick growth ; a clearing with its green
Of emerald Mandioca, then a plain
   Of wild Marsh-rice whence little Reed-birds take
     A happy harvest ;—Mangroves, and once more
    On either side a forest bordered scene
    And seeming endless stretch of Southern shore.

XII.

And far away beyond
  The deep blue Hills that meet the deep blue Skies
    With a more tender blue, and full of thought
Of life, of loss, and gain, and war, and fond
  And tender passion, and all the mysteries
      They bear upon their bosom :—yea, by strife,
    And by its opposite of love, we're brought
    At times to read the mystery of Life !

PALMS AND PARTING DAY.

I.

THE feathery Bamboo makes a delicate Spanish lace
  Of dainty black work traced above a ground of flame,
And the beautiful Palm-trees stretch their fronds and
    meet the place
    With a glorious fern-like fringe that puts Man's work
    to shame.

II.

They stand against the Sunset and lift their wings on
    high
    With never a shadow cast by the glory round on the
    sod,
As Angels stand too rapt for word, or prayer, or cry,
    Silent in adoration before the Heaven of God !

III.

Their pillared stems look lordly ; as a Temple's columns
rise
So rise they, carved and spiral as Solomon's work of
old,
With a flame that shows behind them and broadens across
the skies
As the light caught from the Altar when the clouds of
incense rolled.

IV.

The clinging Orchids on them have caught the golden
glow,
And crimson, orange, and scarlet are cast reflected
back
From the great broad leaves and fingers, and nameless
flowers that grow
To mock all scheme of colour save that in the Sunset's
track.

V.

The Plaintains spread beside them, the broad Banana
sheaves,
The elder fronds in ribbons the younger like shields
of green,
And the Yucca's sombre spear-points where the wild
Vanilla leaves
The higher branch above them to steal their leaves
between.

VI.

And the deep green Stephanotis, with flowers as white as
    the sap
The cut Tree-Rubber gives, trails over the lesser stems,
Where those Humming-birds of dusk, the great grey
    Hawkmoths, tap
The luscious flowers or visit the Cactus diadems.

VII.

The vast dark mass of the Mangoe cuts off a piece from
    view,
    With the Breadfruits' lanceolate leaves, and the dome
    of the Sapotee,
Tho the Jack with its silvery leaf lets the light come
    trickling thro,
    Where the white Convolvulus twines round the laden
    Papaw-tree.

VIII.

But now with the deepened silence comes change in the
    wondrous light,
    And the Bamboo's tracery closes, and the Palms have
    grown more grey,
For the altar fires are fading and the god has sunk from
    sight
    In a dim blue haze that dies in the dusk of parting Day.

STORM STAID.

———◦◦◦———

Up in a Sweet-bean tree, storm staid, I sit
Happy this afternoon, perched up in air,
And, from the tough old trunk I just have climbed,
The shore not ten feet off, with the warm waves
Lipping upon the yellow tropic sand
That, like the long gold of some Sea-Maid's hair,
Lies almost 'neath my feet.—Here round my head
Bright Hornets circle and whiz off, who see
I am no meddler ; and Ichneumon Flies
Settle hard by me, watch me, and arrive
At same conclusions :—now a brilliant flight
Of wee Birds swoop down by me, fearless all,
Who chatter here about me thro the boughs
'Neath which I sit and blink my sleepy eyes
At the bright flakes of sun the sea breeze flicks
Down on me thro the branches, as I loll
Or stretch my limbs like that original Ape
Some hold the Father of our Race.—And I
Picking the Sweet-beans from the tree to eat
The snowy pulp inside, and most content,
Feel not unlike to-day.   Clothed only in

An old and torn and very ragged pair
Of what were once knee-breeches, shorter now
Than when they chased the football, and a shirt
That scarce has kept more than its simple name
Save that 'tis clean, half sleeveless, buttonless,
And free to every wind that finds a way
Thro many a rent and shakes the ragged flannel,—
In tint much like an old Brazilian flag.—

I just have had a warm bath in the sea,
But first, the most of one still sleepy hour,
My naked self lay buried in the sand,
A branch above my head;—the only part
The Sun could reach, the only part the Crabs
Left uninspected and uncrawled upon.

O what it is to feel the great warm Sun
Serve you for clothes for all your nakedness,
The warm sand when you want a coverlid,
The great warm sea, a happy world, wherein
You float, and roll, and swim, and dive, and float,
And then let any wave just take you up
And cast you on the shore and play with you,
A great Sea Mother with her child, until
The Mother Earth fades out, and all you know
Is a happiness that knows not its own joy.—

Below me, far down 'neath me where I sit,
For I am in no weakling baby tree,
The young Palms rise, and older Cocoanuts
Rise higher than myself all round about,
With crowned Pines squatting round about their roots
Broad-boled and sandy; and the Guava trees
That certainly obey great Nature's Law

Be fruitful and increase and spread thy kind,
Mixed with Arnotto trees and the Roselles,
That show a flower-like fruit on every stem
Hold every breath of breeze in fee to kiss.
There a young Cocoanut, say two years old,
With strange large flat and undivided leaf
And most unlike his lordly Parents ; there
Behind Bananas bank the scene that breaks
At times out in a stretch of Sugar-cane.
  To seaward, maybe twenty yards from shore,
Rides our quaint country craft of wondrous rig,
With Piassava ropes and three pole masts,
The fore-mast and the main together stept,
The bowsprit standing straight up in the air.
Enough of it ! Now take the crew : there's one
Coming ashore in our old crank canoe,
As usual hollowed from a single log,
And some of them are dozing 'neath my tree
Wondering what can possess an Englishman
To always risk his neck on any chance
Of climbing higher up a rock or tree.
The rest are lounging round that native hut
Nestling, with others, in this beauteous Bay
That but this morning we for shelter made
From the rough weather out beyond the Bar
That nigh made end of us and craft and crew.—
  The brown Earth round the tree trunk down below,
Trod flat and smooth and hard by frequent feet
Of man and Beast, is littered with the husk
Of man's most common friend thro all the South
The Cocoanut ;—and there a heap of Canes,

But all turned bad, for laziness had changed
Their lazy Cutter's mind, so there they lie
And rot and make rich mould for other growths.—
  There, like great Alligators, in the sun
Bask the long log canoes, three new, one old;
And, like the Creeper that creeps over them,
Now over all there steals a kind of hush.—
  There crows a Cock, and from a distance back
Another answers him, and yet more far
Another crackvoiced bird takes up the crow.
Then all is still again, and the strong tide
Runs like a race up past us from the sea
Filling the long stake nets, perchance, with fish
To furnish evening meals for half the Folk.
  An old Sow waddles from behind the house
And pitches on the litter of the pods
Dropt from my eating, grunting now and then
A meditation on their excellence.
  Now on that sail spread out to air and dry
One of the house dogs comes and lays himself,
And, tho my bare white legs a moment take
His thought and eye, he feels too lazy far
For any barking; and 'twixt him and me
A spider slowly lets himself slip down
From his strong thread, and swings there in the wind
For some good reason, I suppose, but known
Only to him as far as I can say.
  A solitary Ant goes hurrying up
The great bough where I sit on some concern
Of deep import, her pace can not be less
Than sixty miles an hour if taken in

Proportion to her size.—A smaller Pig
Has now come out to forage round my tree,
And there, almost full-fed, the elder Swine,
Contentment oozing out from every pore,
Rubs her black hide against a standing post.—
The younger Pig chews o'er the Sugar cane,
Already once chewed well by man below,
Munches the Mangoe skins sucked clean of fruit,
Routing thro Orange peel and Soursops
On which some other has worked before poor
    Pig.—
But there he has a prize, a bit of Jack,
Doubtless half rotten, but then Jack is Jack
At least to Pigs, who in that litter there
Are bound to pick up something ; Papaw rinds,
And Limes, and Plantains, Sapotees, and bits
Of sickly Custard-Apple.—Two bright eyes look
Up at me from below ; that Lizard wants
To pass me on this bough and higher climb
For love or sport :—for sport, I see the fly.
Just look at him, what coolness, using me
To stalk his prey, he makes the final spring
From my bare knee, and, lo, he has Sir Buz !—
Holds him quite still, a gulph, a gulph, a gulph,
His lunch is down, and now he gives three clucks
Almost like some old sitting Hen and slips
A few feet higher up into the sun.

  I somehow feel all creatures know me well
And that I will not hurt them, and the trust
Is well repaid. I never have been stung,
Or bitten, living in their very midst.

The world is more to me than other men
But not for anything the world can give,
But simply for the fact it is the world
And full of life ; and with what face you look
Upon the world the world refaces you,
Act and react is its great Law ; the love
That flows out from you must flow back again
Or were the balance wrong, and hence . . . but now
The Sun has made more west, and thro the leaves
The slanting rays strike gentler on my limbs,
And his broad face blinks thro the Cocoanut groves
Across the Bay, and, as the Eve comes down,
I too come down with Evening to the shore !

PIGMY PAMPAS.

———◆◇◆——— .

I.

THIS is never a Prairie but yet the air is calm
  And holy and still and sweet and warm with the tropic
  sun,
Where, hardly felt in its passing, the breeze goes over in
  balm
  And the leaves scarce move to greet it before its course
  is run.

II.

The blue Hills rise to the right, to the left the line of the
  Seas,
  Stretches of grass lands lying before us and falling away
Into the blue dim distance, that dies in a dreamland of
  trees
  Mystic before and behind us that rise and that end
  with the day.

III.

Not just a great green waste like the endless Plains of
　　the South,
　　Pampas as bare as the Desert, for the eye grows weary
　　　of grass,
But a place of beautiful Insects, and Birds with a song in
　　the mouth,
　　And many a happy life that slips from your path as you
　　　pass.

IV.

Here a deep pool hidden by a dense green growth of
　　Reeds
　　That up to their knees in water stand whispering back
　　to the banks,
Where the Lilies flap their leaflets and open their cups,
　　and the Weeds
　　For a moment rise from the ripples to answer the tale in
　　thanks.

V.

In the sand of the path we are treading the Ants are busy
　　and brief
　　Working each in his way and working each with a will,
Every slave in the Army carrying a great green leaf
　　Marshalled along by their chiefs in a line to the distant
　　Hill.

VI.

And the Spider stretches above them her net with its
  diamond dew
  Flashing from every knot whereon she toiled thro the
    dark,
And striking into our sense from a speck in the limitless
  blue
  Comes a Bird's note with a touch in its trill of our
    English Lark.

VII.

Here a patch of Palm, and the Piassava flings
  Its half closed hands in the air like a strong Man
    stretching his arms,
And all about the branches you hear a breeze that sings
  For a Palm can never whisper a secret to other
    Palms.

VIII.

Not like the Forest leaves that hardly seem to shake
  But yet tell all their neighbours the story the wind has
    told,
For, tho the Palms are older, far better have Wood and
  Brake
  Learned that to chatter is silver but a soft low voice is
    gold.

IX.

And here in the patch of Woodland we are passing upon
    the right,
    Where the trees are heavy with Creepers and their
        wonderful cups hang down,
And the Orchids cover the branches with many a marvel-
    lous sight
    Of Flowers as Fairies fragile or quaint as a Circus
        Clown

X.

The delicate Humming-Bird flashes, the golden Oriel sits,
    The scarlet Oriel scolds with Parroquets thro the
        boughs,
And a thousand nameless beauties of Wrens, and Robins,
    and Tits,
    Settle disputes, and mate, and match, and marry, and
        house.—

     *   *   *   *   *

XI.

The Snake hangs from the branches and swings him to
    and fro
    And his slate-blue tongue flicks out an instant from his
        jaws,
With an eye that keeps good watch on the well trod path
    below
    Waiting the Treader's coming :—we both are under His
        laws

XII.

And take what good God gives us; no doubt 'tis hard to
read
  When you think that that little Creature has tasted of
  light and good,
And here, by the hand of its Maker, is being led up to
bleed
  And serve with this only end in life as the Serpent's
  food.

XIII.

How in its agony fear and death can it cry to God,
  Who, ruling by law, has given the poor thing over to
  Death.—
And the very Sparrows are numbered, and our hairs, and
  the grass of the sod,
  Unsearchable, deep are His ways in the giving and
  taking of breath !

XIV.

But God is good I know, and He reigns, I know it, and
feel
  That things are so, if he was not good, no God could
  reign,
But the mystery here is so great I stand unable to kneel
  Silent before the unsearchable secret of sin and of
  pain.

XV.

But the grand Sun rides overhead in a blue sky, blue
    without spot,
  And the great blue Sea goes stretching as spotless away
    from my sight,
We are glorious and pure, and we work, nor are troubled
    what is and is not,
  For a Greater than both is above us the end of whose
    actions is right !

A SHORE SCENE.

I.

THE tide has run asea
   And here we wait, and half upon our side,
     With other little vessels in the Port.—
Look there across the mud, there seems to be
   Some little stir on by that shop : his hide
       The old Pig scratches softly, listening well
   To hear his Master's squabble, as with sort
       Of umpire grunt he chews that fruit that fell,

II.

Where underneath the trees
   Stand the small houses, white-washed and dark-tiled,
     With here and there a patch, late introduced,
Of newer red tile : often too one sees,
   Where hard by gambols many a naked child,
       Cracked walls that show bright brick-red wattle
        and dab,
     From which by the fierce tropic rain-pour sluiced
       The lime has fallen away in many a slab.

III.

The windows gay with paint.—
    Round many a door a bright red streak is drawn,
    Round others a bright blue, and all the wood
Between the bands shows an ' æsthetic' taint,
    Bright pea-green 'harmonies,' and with them borne
        Bright yellow, and your poor teeth get on edge
      Till your eyes wander on and see how good
      Harmonious Nature is in that old hedge.

IV.

We've nearly done with man,
    Thank Goodness, here, save that he's tried in vain,
    Too lazy to work well, a little pier
Out from the shore, for, when his stone blocks ran
    Too far and sunk, he never tried again
        To get them up, but calmly let them be :
      And there they wait and slowly year by year
      The long tides drag them deeper out to sea.

V.

One straggling little street
    Behind a bank of broad Banana leaves
      Backed by two Breadfruit, with their leaves deep cut
And marked so strong that at three hundred feet
    The sight their most peculiar shape receives,
        And seeing there their round rough-rinded fruit
      That in the great House as in the humblest Hut
      Is well appreciated by man and brute.

VI.

Straggling to right and left
 Rise a few Coacoanuts ; and like sisters stand
  Three tall Arecas, fairest Palm-trees there,
That, after many a year from Time is reft
 And slow development has moved the Land,
  Above a fountain where the gossips talk,
  Will front, what then will be the Public Square
  And hear the Band play by the Public walk.

VII.

But that has all to come.—
 Around our " Yacht " some dozen other crafts
  Wait too the tide : some loading wood and oil,
Cacoa, farinha, cordage, pottery some,
 And some discharging boilers cranks and shafts
  Bought for some great Engenho as it seems,
  But such deliberation in their toil
  They look as if they only worked in dreams.

VIII.

The Plantain leaves about
 Are very ragged, 'tis a sign of wind,
  And in the Launcha next our own the men
Are looking thro their sails and cordage stout.—
 An Anchor yesterday we left behind
  And had a nasty struggle with the gale,
  I should not care for that lee-shore again
  And those five minutes of a doubtful sail.

IX.

Farinha and Jerked-Beef,
     Add too Black-beans, and you have all their food
          With Fish and Fruit, but yonder on the shore
See the one shop, owned by a gentle Thief,
     Whose prices must be paid ere understood :
          And these Folk must have money, for they buy,
     And Customers are always at the Store,
          And all the things are English probably.

X.

Except the bottled "Bass."
     The Beer is German, and the labels sent
          Out by an enterprising German Firm.
And nothing can be done to stop this, as
     "Curtis and Harvey" find with discontent
          Their own tins filled with Powder and retailed.
     You wonder, and repress the angry term,
          Seeing their trusty brand with you has failed.

XI.

Loafing about the shore,
     And both apparently intent on Crab,
          Go Pigs and Goats, and marvellously like,
Perhaps their common food has caused this, or
     Some cause unknown ; no Dog will make a grab
          At any legs, for, far too lazy, all
     Lie in the Sun, and you must smartly strike
          Before they to some other spot will crawl.

XII.

Man too gets just as mixed
  As do the Animals, for Black and White
    Seem trying hard to make one common Race
Of Whitey-Brown, and building up betwixt
  Them both a supreme plainness : streaks of light
      At times appear,—here comes the English barque,
    The Yankee Schooner, and you meet a face
    That shows a touch of Saxon in the dark.

XIII.

The long black crank Canoes,
  The common Dug-outs lie about the mud
    Like Alligators on some River strand :
Here a small Nigger, minus clothes or shoes,
  Paddles a wee one down, a boat in bud,
      'Tis just an old one cut in two, a board
    Nailed o'er the end, the first that came to hand,
    Whereon he sits as happy as a Lord.

XIV.

There from the Sapotee
  The ripe fruit drops, the fruitful Plantain bends
    Beneath its load, the bountiful Papaw
Is thick with fruit as thick as stem can be,
  The Yam trails on and on, and never ends
      The Sweet-potatoe-vine's Convolvulus ;
    Add fifty fruits, no tithe of what you saw,
    What need of work when Nature worketh thus.
        *   *   *   *   *

XV.

I'm sure you'd like Brazil
  If you care just to sit on Nature's lap,
    And take whate'er she gives you from her breast,
Starving, or feeding freely at her will,
    Taking no thought of what may chance to hap.—
      And this Folk's Sire's held half the World in fee—
     I'd sooner keep our roaring strong North West
      Than all their Lotos of this Southern Sea !

THE LEGEND OF LILITH.

TO
TERESA COLONNA,
Duchess of Marino.

My dear Duchess,—At Merton some few months ago, as I was sketching out my idea of "Lilith" and the application of the Legend to the life that we have to-day, you asked me to write you a longer Poem upon the mysterious Lady :—you see I have now done so and dedicate it to its true Author, trusting she will always remain the same kindly and sympathetic Critic that she has been hitherto.

Faust. Who is that yonder?

Mephistopheles. Mark her well. It is.
  Lilith.

Faust. Who?

Mephistopheles. *Lilith*, the first wife of *Adam*.

FAUST.—Shelley's Translation.

In regard to my ' Lilith ' of a former Volume as well as to the subject and matter of this present Poem, with the exception of the few suggestive lines from *Goethe's* Faust, quoted on the foregoing page, I have had to rely absolutely upon my imagination, and upon my observation of those feelings, for the most part hidden, but that at times are more or less made manifest in the lives of all of us. And tho here some may forget, I expect that none grow up beneath the tree of life without this knowledge ; for as well as men do women have these thoughts, or let me rather call them instincts, and, being of higher nature and finer fibre, are even more sensitive to the whisper of

> That dim Adam whose faint face is
> Fairest to the young girl's dreams
> In the wilds of vanished places
> Till his haunting presence seems
> Someone she has lost, and only
> Known far back in other years
> Ere the world had found her lonely
> With a song still in her ears,

And for us men, who have for the most part to meet the world full face and are earlier thrown against the thorns and thistles outside that fair Garden, there swim up strange beliefs and unaccountable memories of

> That Face, that Face that rules our inner life
> And comes between us and all other faces !

THE LEGEND OF LILITH.

———◦◦———

" Thou art of other Lands than these of ours,
   O Love, O Love, that risest up between
   Myself and all the Fairest I have seen
On this dull world ! " * * * A Year of Life, cxxi.

In that old Garden of the Orient
I hold it truth our first of life is spent,
Before the life that cometh after birth
Takes us to dree the tangled doom of Earth.—
   There is one Face more than all other Faces
That we hold holy, and in quiet places
Of earth and sea and in thought's central deeps
It ever haunts us ; and its presence keeps
About us memories, whose half opened lips
Whisper of things that were, until there slips
Upon us that dim moment when we meet
An instant here our Lady sad and sweet,
Half Girl, half Wife ; and on each Maid doth wait
A Being, half God, and half remembered Mate :
For Woman hath her Adam that nigh filleth
The void this Earth makes ; all men have their Lilith ;
And none that know life and its mysteries

Escape the power of those twin Presences.
And here I write the Legend that hath risen
From foolish Dark Age dreams that, as in prison,
Hold in the thought, that in all hearts hath taken
Some germ or rise the moment hearts awaken
And find expression ; frequent more or less
In speech of gold or silver, but whose dress
Has often hidden so the spoken word
That men half listen or but dream they heard.

    GOD who made all things here, this world of ours,
The Creeper tendril, and the painted Flowers,
The Humming-bird, the delicate Butterflies,
The Golden Suns, the Peacock's feathered eyes,
Who made all nature since his Word began
To work and make made last and greatest Man !
Lord of all things below, He set him there
Perfect and placed where all things else were fair.
Alone he stood preeminent and grew,
As grow the Palms, more strong from dew to dew,
And drank in knowledge as the Wax-tree drinks
When deeply through the sand its taproot sinks
To reach the hidden water-springs below :—
The more he learned the more he sought to know
For all things told their tale, and evermore
Their tales grew sweeter than those told before.
Each Leaf, each Insect came to him for name,
The Golden Oriel, a flash of flame,
The Eagle and the Wren, the Ant, the Bee,
The nimble Ape that swung from tree to tree,
The Bear, the Lion, and the spotted Pard,

The Bison with his frontlet stony hard
And horns that meet across his brows, the Snake
And the bright Lizard from the tangled brake,
The patient Ox that knew not then the yoke,
The Dog Man's Friend that all has done but spoke,
The Wader Birds, the Fish that held the deep,
The Moths of evening and the Bats of sleep,
Creatures of land and river, sea and air,
Changed now, poor things, but still how very fair,
How fairer then before fell rapine smote
Their instinct here and took them by the throat
And forced them on to slaughter, and to prey
Greater or weaker as they do to-day.
But then were all things perfect without jar,
And this mild Earth, centre of many a Star
That watched it lovingly, basked in the rays
Of a kind circling Sun that made its days.—
  So Adam grew in solitary state
From light to light, but for him was no mate
Found in his vast domain; but everything
Was yet so new no moment felt the King
The loss all Nature disapproves, and he
Ruled on alone in lonely majesty,
Content with self and with the World around
Till sudden came the thought, for me is found
No Mate, no Mate, and stronger yet the thought
Grew on him day by day, who ever sought
Thro hill and vale, and thro the shady groves,
Whose leaves the breeze to dream of loving moves,
And thro the plains, and by the whispering seas,
That one loved Presence of all Presences.—

Why am I speechless, who alone can speak,
Having no one to answer ! Lo ! the meek
Eyed Dove can murmur to his brooding Mate,
The Heath·fowl crows to where his Hen doth wait,
The Stag calls to his Hinds, the Tigress
Roars back an answer to her Lord, the Ness
And Cape re-echo to the Sea-birds' call
To their wild Mates at sea, for each and all
Some dear Companion waits whose life and life
Makes but one Being, only for me no Wife.—
Whence is it :—wherefore am I Lord of all
If there is none whom I my Queen may call,
Vain Monarch of vain Empire, all is vain,
Would life, would I could cease to be again !
  So plained he in his loneliness, and near
The Devil, ever watching, glad to hear
Formed deep resolve. For he had seen High God
Form Adam from the red-earth of the sod,
Mold him, and fashion him, and make him fair
In His own image, ere he placed him there
Filled with the breath of God which was his soul,
Made part thus of the universal whole,
Which, in the end, from every growth and clod
Is rendered back to Universal God !—
There hearing Adam plain the Devil went,
On that wild errand he will aye repent,
Back to the very spot from which God drew
The dust of Adam : molding therewith too
The fairest Creature that He could conceive.
With subtle brain He did about her weave
All beauty and all loveliness for dress,

E

Upon her fashioning each golden tress
Of the Sun's glory; from the shell her foot,
Pink-edged and perfect; took of Nature's lute,
The wind among the rushes, for her voice,
The which to only hear would make rejoice
The dullest heart of Man; her eyebrows drawn
Clear as the mountains when they cut the Dawn;
Her eyes were full of loves, and fears, and hopes,
As are deep pools of water; when it opes
The red pomegranate shows her lips; her teeth
Were like the milky quartz that far beneath
Some mountain range is thrust; her chin,—but there
Words are vain things, enough that she was fair.
A loveliness itself made visible
Whereon the love of Man for aye might dwell,
Ah! not for aye;—for, tho he made her whole
Fair body perfect, that great gift of soul
Was not within her Maker's gift. But he
Was filled with pride. I am Divinity
What can God make more perfect, as this Maid
The Man himself is not so fair, he said !—
    That night in sleep our common Father lay
When a deep dream of bliss fell on him; say
Have you—and you no dreams?—Ah! Adam had
A dream that made life new and all things glad;
He trembled in his sleep lest he should wake;
He trembled lest the day should come and break
His vision till it passed and ceased to be—
He woke and found it was reality!
None can describe that hour, that meeting, all
Remembrance of it vanished at the Fall,

Save that to all his Children in their dreams
Comes some remembrance, but in fitful gleams.
    So Adam lived and loved, where with him dwelt
That Fairy Being, at whose feet he knèlt
At first in very worship, giving not
To God the praise, for God he said forgot
His creature here until this other came
And made my life no longer only name.—
And as time passed upon its onward way
Were children born unto them, fair were they,
Half human and half not. Born without soul
But with a yearning deep for it, their goal
Since then till now ; a hundred years their term
Of life on earth, with but in them the germ
Of immortality ; if they could gain
Another soul to love them, not in vain
Had they a human Father, for this love
Would give a spirit to them, and above
They might live on for ever ; but, if not,
They bade farewell unto each well loved spot,
Roamed one last time the glades they loved to roam,
Then ceased to be as bubbles of the foam.
But that was long years hence : the Elves and Fays
Were children still, and scarce knew many days
When on their Father came a change. For Lilith,
The Mate he had, not all Man's being filleth ;
Tho one with soul may mate with one without
'Tis not for long, at last there comes about
The cry that gains no answer in the place
She cannot fill :—and, as the good God's face
Is full of mercy, he heard Adam's cry

Who knew not half his prayer, and suddenly
As in a dream his Lilith passed away
To be seen never more, for so men say,
Save thro her Babes; but kept, for God is good,
In a mild Land, where not one wind is rude,
And wherein all is peace, save that in dreams
She sees her Adam, and he often seems
To be awhile beside her, but whose might
Is scarce more than some half-remembered night
Of happy visions : and she sits and waits
Until, perchance, those present half-closed gates
Are opened wider, and there cometh ONE
Thro whom her entrance shall be made and done !—
    But upon Adam a deep sleep there fell
Deep as is Death's whence none return to tell
What things may be : and of his very bone
And flesh God fashioned One for him alone,
Solely for him created, life of life,
Distinct and marked with holy name of Wife,
And full of soul from God, made to receive
All love and give it back, whose name was Eve,
Mother of all of us ; and of all since
The fairest Fair, as Adam, Sire and Prince,
Doubtless surpassed his Sons : for all their Gifts
Descend from him, whose single greatness lifts
Him past comparison.   And in God's Garden dwelt
The Parents of all men, and daily knelt
Each thanking God for gift of each in bliss
Of perfect purity and happiness.
But still persistent there,—as constant climbs
The Parasite up the Tree that oftentimes

Sheds bark and casts the tendril down to climb
With patience up again another time
Until it holds the stem and masters it,—
The Devil ever strove, dismayed no whit,
To merit the name Tempter; as he went
At times did Adam feel a discontent,
And came dim memories back·: the Dæmon saw
The growing thought, and ever whispered more
Of her of old, and Adam moved apart
To ponder on these whisperings of the heart
Leaving his Eve alone, the weaker one
To be by this sad fantasy sore undone.
For to her flew the Devil : thro the brake
He sought some instrument and found the Snake,
A wondrous form and wise, and him possessed
And straight him to his evil work addressed
With cruel craft.   Eve sat beneath that tree
Whose fruit was fair, and that hung gloriously
Above from laden boughs to where the cool
Deep river showed her mirrored in the pool
In lonely beauty ; wondering for her Mate,
His strange desertion sad and desolate,
And wondering if her beauty had grown less,
Then smiling happy at her loveliness
And conscious of its glory, and then sad
For loss of Adam in those fits he had
Of dreamy single wandering.—Ah ! most Fair—
The Serpent sighed.   Eve started, hearing there
A Serpent speak. Whence hast thou voice she cried ?
Thy beauty gave it me, he straight replied,
Thy beauty Queen of Eden ;—and thy Mate

Wanders afar, and sad and desolate
Leaves thee his Spouse: stretch forth thy hand and eat
From the Tree of Wisdom, fruitful to thy feet,
And thou wilt gain all knowledge, and wilt bring
Straight to thy side once more thy Lord and King.
  Not so, said Eve, for He who placed us here
Gave us all fruit to eat save this, I fear
His word and I obey, and straight I charge thee, Wife,
Hath Adam said, this and the Fruit of Life
Thou shalt not eat, so are we bade of God.—
Whereat the Serpent lifting from the sod
Its glittering head. O gentle, guileless Bride,
Well the device hath to thee been applied !
God added, did He not, that thou shouldst die
The day thou did'st eat. I have eaten, I —
So from the first as ever he hath lied—
Have eaten, and behold I have not died
But gained the power, when I thy beauty saw
To tell thee of my worship, who before
Had worshipped thee in silence ! That fruit did teach
Me wisdom, yea, and gifted me with speech,
Thou art my Queen, thy King is absent, where,
Why hath he left thee ? Is there other fair
As thou art beautiful ? Who can answer ! There
Alone lies all reply, and wisdom given
To all who taste that pregnant fruit of Heaven !—
He ceased and soon the venom of his speech
Worked to her heart, and made her fingers reach
A golden apple from the bending bough.
But it dropped idly from her, for not now
Was the sad moment come, and by her lay

Thro all the long noon of that fatal day.
And Lilith, as in a dream and wonder-eyed,
With lips half pitiful passed by her side,
Half conscious of the future and in part
Having that hopeless hunger in the heart
That we inherit, till the evening light
Took her into itself and closed the sight.
And Eve, who could not see her, when she went
Felt sorrow on her soul, and discontent
The while the Serpent plied her, whispering well
Until she tasted it, and Woman fell !
And Adam found her, and found in his Wife
That love and loss that make the gain of life
When that life comes that shall be after this.
And of the fruit Eve gave him with her kiss,
Dear Eve, her Daughters ever since have given
The same with love and anguish, loss and Heaven,
So strangely mixed in one ! Ah God ! to think
How long we paused neith ere we crossed the brink,
The fatal brink of one sad fall, the skies
And gardens of eternal Paradise.
From hence but little speech may tell the tale :—
The Angel-guarded Eden ; and the wail
Of ruined Creatures ; and the flaming swords ;
A just God's stern but mercy tempered words ;
The Thistles and the Thorns these thousand years
Still hold about us ; and the Heaven that hears
The cry of Abel's blood, and all the vain
And impotent regret of God-marked Cain !

Such in dim outline seems it Men did hold

The legend of fair Lilith, loved of old
By our first Father Adam : but I deem
Ours is a different Lilith, and none dream
Such strange and vivid dreams save they have known
Their dreams the truth in times that long have flown.
　　I hold, some how, that every one of us,
Whose birth into this world is marvellous
And beyond reason, in a former state
Hath lived and loved and known their proper Mate.
Somehow this world seems but a link between
A world to be and one that long hath been
But that still haunts us in this life, in these
Strange fields, with Memories and dim Presences,
But that are strong, for all we cannot grasp
Their hands, or hold them to our breast, or clasp
Our arms about their necks.　Each Man here has
Someone that is his Lilith, and that was
His Mate in that old World ; and every Maid
Her Adam, a dim Adam that doth fade
With change and years of life, but yet whose hand
Is on her bosom should she musing stand
O'er all the Past, and over her young year
Of life, when, may be, fell upon her ear
The voice of someone she had loved and known,
And her heart stirred in answer to its own.
Can one explain this ; whence this feeling grows !
Hence, from this unexplained, the Legend rose.
How God made Adam, placed in Eden fair
Alone to gain all knowledge that was there ;
How that the Devil, working in despite,
Brought to him Lilith in a dream of night ;

And how they lived, and how that from them sprung
The Elves and Fairies known to every tongue ;
And how God's wrath did shortly separate
His Creature, Adam, from that soulless Mate,
And pitiful, in that he saw him grieve,
Made him forget her and created Eve,
Who, being tempted, fell, whereat both lost
Their former glory to our bitter cost.—
Yes, such the Legend, foolish in its way,
But yet with a deep truth in it I say,
For has not each his Lilith ?   Does no face
Bring up that other of the older Place ?
Does not some scene recall some older scene,
And well, I know, you say, that this hath been,
This, this, I saw, and this, and this, and then
The memory swims off, leaving you again
Hopeless of answer, and of space to meet
That one loved face, that Lady sad and sweet,
Half girl half wife !   Ah well, some thing may be
In all the long years yet to roll that we
Stand guessing at so vainly !   Ah, dim guessing,
Wherein we know not if we are transgressing,
Or if our shafts of thought take proper curve
Drawn with sure aim, or with some thoughtless swerve
Drawn at a venture ; as they leave the string,
Like that old arrow, will they smite the King
Until he turn his chariot from the press
And give us answer where we now but guess ?
Who knows ! Who knows ! We are but playthings here
Tossed up and caught again from year to year :
At times the Great Hand misses us, we fall,

But conscious that a GREATER over all
Is keeping watch ; that spite of us, that spite
Of all the lesser gods, is infinite
In its perfections and makes every fall
And slip, if we fall facing over all
That far-off light, a stumble that will lift
Us higher yet, and to more perfect gift
Of Manful walking.   Children here as yet,
We cry because the crowning coronet
Was not born with us, and is but attained
After hard toil along the road, and pained
For imminent rocks and rocks that fall and bruise
Both head and shoulders.   We have much to lose
And have lost much, but aye have more to gain,
And after all this mockery sore and vain,
And after all this present strife and ill,
Must make some harbour, where the granite hill
Behind outstretches both its arms to keep
The quiet waters in a gentle sleep.
On those blest shores, to other meaning won,
These words can be writ down, dispute of none,
Beneath the brooding summer still of Heaven,
Silent as are that mystic starry Seven,
Endless, and sweet as the soft breath of Even,
As each long year its happy moments filleth,
Each hath her Adam all men have their Lilith !—

FOR T. C.

————◦◇◦————

A TOUCH of ice makes tardy this our Spring,
   Sheds the white blossoms down like snowflakes fast,
   Breaks the young buds off, grim Iconoclast,
And takes sad tithe of every lovely thing.—
Life has its winters and its cold snows cling
   About the heart, and, as the days o'er past
   Rise one by one, each crueller than the last,
We feel its bitter frost, remembering
     Those summer glories over-gone and spent.—
       Yet peace, the new Sun rises over all;
     Tardy, maybe, but on sure mission sent
       By ONE whose good works on thro grime and gall.—
     In that old Garden of the Orient
       Full well I know there was no frost and fall!

DIVINE DEATH.

Of all the demi-gods is quiet Death
  The most divine ; for none can stand his might,
  Who cometh on resistless as the Night
And hath the cold of Darkness in his breath.—
He holds in fee the whole World, and none saith
  " What dost thou here in Lands thou hast no right ? "—
  But as Nights darkness breaks in Morning light,
So Death brings Life, and Man but slumbereth !
    As Children here we fear the night and dark
      With a blind childish fear that doubts and cries,
    Unthinking some great Father aye must mark
      Each movement with a Father's pitying eyes,
    And watching some small taper's transient spark
      Unmindful of the great Sun to arise !

SOMEONE.

I.

—◦◦◦—

TALK of blue Italian skies—
Ah, the deeper blue that lies
In the depth of Woman's eyes !

Never coral from the South
Like the coral of her mouth
When the Woman comes on Youth.—

Ah, the dainty chin whose curve
With a delicate reserve
Tells of rule that waits to serve !

And the ripple of the ear
That takes in the meaning clear
Of the tides that tend more near.

Hers a voice as soft and low
As the silver over flow
Where the slender streamlets go.

Never yet across the brink
Of the Day did Morn, I think,
Fingers lift so dainty pink.

Never Mountain cut the Dawn
With a brow so deftly drawn
As those o'er her eyelids borne.

Talk of form,—as grand and calm
Stands the Queen-Areca Palm
In a breath of Southern balm !

Talk of Soul,—Ah ! turn and mark
Vega's bright ætherial spark
Glittering on the breast of Dark—

Vega of the Heavenly Lyre,
Would my lips could touch its fire—
Lend thine Eagle wings Altair !

ADSUM.

II.

O NORTH wind waken from thy rest,
  O South blow softly from the South,
Come passionate East, and O thou West
  Draw near and kiss her on the mouth !

Breathe on her Gardens, let the spice
Of many a balmy scent be shed,
And without count, or cost, or price,
Pour Springs best odours on her head !

She sleeps !—Then wake her gentle Breeze,
Whichever hearken to my call,
With low sweet murmuring thro the trees
Like babbling waters half hushed fall.

She sleeps !—Ah no ! She sleepeth not !
Her heart awakened waits my sight,
Who sought her long and unforgot
Thro plains and dewy fields of Night.

O Night farewell ; now only day
Where thou art waiting Love for me :
Tho sorely wounded on the way
I come to thee ! I come to thee !

PLIGHTED.
III.

BEFORE great God the Father of us both
That makes the love that rises in us two,
I swear that henceforth I am true to you
By that which binds men more than any oath :—
And freely I come to you, and not loth

To lose this aimlessness in what I do,
This wild life—wandering without end or view,
This gainless haste or most unseemly sloth.
    And you—Love is not Love that spends his cry
        With piteous plain for entrance at the heart—
    Rose up with new waked wonder in your eye
        For all your power, ne'er brought to public mart,
    Stretched out your arms and took him tenderly,
        And henceforth from the World we walked apart !

FOR A TRIPTYCH, BY HERBERT SCHMALZ.

———◆———

I.

THE STILL SILENT PAST.

THE Past is still and silent, and ' nomore '
  Is the one word the Past can ever say ;
  Her fires are embers, and the light of day
Is almost faded from her desolate shore :
About her lie dead bones that were of yore
  For joy and life, and flowers with leaves grown grey,
  And rivers parched whose streams have passed away,
And ruined cities where men dwelt before.
    Dead darnels stand about her, sapless roots
     And buds with petals gone, about her rise
    Reeds no winds shake and wan unwatered shoots.—
     Yet beauty still is hers, dreamless she lies,
    Since, when he saw her withered flowers and fruits,
     Death pitying stooped and kissed her on the eyes !

F

II.

THE DIM MYSTIC FUTURE.

Dim lies the Past behind you, in dim light
   The solemn cypress rise along the strand,
   And the tall poplars in that ghostly Land
Whose river stretches winding out of sight.—
The Present lies about you, but its might
   Is not upon you, and its running sand
   Glitters unnoticed round you where you stand,
Who holdest the Present at its worth aright.
      Here, Sweet, behind you burns the moon ; on Star
         Above your head, a little lambent spark ;
      The touch and token of the thing you are,
         A halo faint Men rather feel than mark ;
      Great eyes that look out trustfully afar
         To take the hidden message of the dark.

III.

THE PRESENT BITTER-SWEET.

Languid and heavy-lidded, yet withal
   A strange light in her eyes, and on her lips
   A strange sad smile ; beyond her slide the ships
Upon the river ; voices rise and fall ;
Folk come and go, but, thro the palm-leaves tall
   And roses and lilies, shown in dim eclipse :
   From string to string her lute-worn finger slips
With sounds half sad and half not musical.

On a rich seat of state she takes her ease,
   Seeing, perchance, her Lovers at her feet,
And few there are of men she counts not these.—
   Thy symbols are the heart that makes complete
Thy neck-worn beads, thy fountained terraces,
   O passionless Queen! O Present bitter-sweet!

FINAL.

The Past, the Present, and the Future make
   But one, that not to be conceived thing,
   Eternity, that with all shadowing wing
Encompasseth the earth. We cannot take
The thought in, that whatever word doth break
   The still about us here doth move a string
   That vibrates on for ever, and will ring
Its story thro all Space. When we awake
     From sleep to read our life here, we will see
     No other page before us but the page
That lies now round us, that continually
     We put harsh pen to on our pilgrimage.—
O vain to babble in Eternity
     Of Past, or Present, or of Future Age!

THE OAK ROOM.

OXBOROUGH HALL, 20TH JANUARY, 1885.

I.

THIS is the Ghost-haunted chamber and the Lady sweet
and stately
Looks down lovely from her canvass, Lady tell the
tale you had,
I am ready for your visit, comprehend your liquid
Spanish,
Or if you should use the poet language of the Luisiad.

II.

All that beauty has its story, not the cruel tide of passion,
Something sweet and most pathetic; yours is not an
Angel-face
Good or bad, but just a Woman's, grand, indeed, but
still a Woman's,
With your columned neck and shoulders rising thro a
foam of lace.

III.

Born to Southward,—I too like you,—by the Minho or
    Najarrha,.
  And your thoughts go wandering homeward from this
    English home of yours
To the orange groves of Seville. " Ætat." "Ætat twenty
    three !"
  Ah, those darling days of fancy; sad that Art alone
    endures !

IV.

These three hundred years have left you with the pink
    upon your cheek
  Ripe and warm and dainty coloured from the kisses of
    the South,
But for all your girlish beauty and the simple look about
    you
  You've a history somewhere hidden round the corners
    of your mouth.

V.

Something draws my eyes towards you back from where
    soe'er they wander,
  Back once more with sweet compulsion till my sight
    upon you rests,
Making poor the touch of Reubens and the bountiful
    ambition
  To display her limbs and shoulders of that Venus with
    the breasts.

VI.

Other Ladies look down on me, fair enough that Lady
    yonder,
  Peeping, woman-like and curious, o'er the solemn
    candlesticks ;
And that other calm and holy, Nunlike almost in her
    beauty,
  Holding in her thin white fingers still the jewelled
    crucifix.

VII.

Yonder " Mrs. Booth "—her maiden name is written
    " Hester Santlon."—
  Actress doubtless, very pretty, reigning in her day as
    Queen,
With her gold-hair and her black eyes, and complexion,
    like a roseleaf,
  Lips like rosebuds too half open with some snow that
    shows between.

VIII.

Saintly Ladies some and sober, others gay and young and
    gladsome,
  Laughing from the walls or hanging o'er the carved
    oak chimney piece ;—
How the carvings mope and chatter, as the failing fire
    flames flicker,
  Ye are all but dreams and fancies soon to cease as we
    shall cease.

IX.

Ah, but no, there comes an answer from your deep dark
 eyes my Lady,
  And a whisper fills the chamber and thro all my being
  slips,
Making sure that crumb of comfort that remains tho all
 else vanish
  Sealed for certain by the solemn voiceless language of
  your lips !

X.

Yes, the past is like the future, both are someday to be
 known,
  Both are staid and both are silent, here none read
  their horoscope,
Save for one sweet word that trembles on the lips that
 scarce dare name it,
  Cheering present, past, and future, where you whisper
  dear of " Hope."

IN MEMORIAM.

HENRY FAWCETT, born 1833, died 1884.

———◦◦◦———

He was my Friend who never saw my face,
  The blind man trusted me, and I, a Boy,
  Was well content to enter his employ
For meed of each day's thanks.—Ah! lovely Place
The light has faded from you, and the grace,
  And from your woods the kindling soul and joy,
  The shadow of *two* deaths on you destroy
Some certain lines naught earthly could erase.—
    Take this world's Baals :—tho all People cried
      Them gods, I know this man would ne'er have knelt.
    Does truth count ought, then this man never lied ;
      Truth like anointing flame upon him dwelt.—
    There are not many Fawcetts ; when he died
      Men hardly realized the loss they felt !

IN MEMORIAM.

1885.

My Namesake,—doubtless too of common blood ;—
  It is our pride that every Highland name
  Holds all the kindred of that Clan the same,
And our name, Kinsman, not the last has stood
Upon our Country's rolls of hardihood
  In ranks of fight and deathful fields of flame ;
  But thine a harder not less noble fame,
O Soldier of the Pen renowned and good !
    Yea, loss more great than England's treasure spent
      Is Herbert, worthy of old Carnarvon ;
    And that great lonely Soul, betrayed and pent
      By circling Foes, who as the days went on
    Felt daily he must die ere aid was sent ;—
      And with these two thy loss, young Cameron !

ENGLAND.   APRIL, 1885.

———◆———

Now let the banner of England blow once more out on
    the breeze
For the winds of the North have caught it and the breath
    of the Southern seas,
And the limitless West hath spoken and the lands that
    lie to the East
That cry, There are bonds between us that have slack-
    ened but have not ceased ;
We are Children of one great Mother who was grand in
    the making of men,
Who was mighty in moulding the Nations, and who shall
    be mighty again.
    Let the dead Past bury its dead and its stumbles and
    failures and bring
Into the life of the Future its lights, and each glorious
    thing
That made us the People we are, not insular, Folk of a
    Place,
But part in that People's progression that only can end
    with the Race

That is English and not to be conquered !—Is it just, is
    it fair, that the Sons
Should not have the rights of the Fathers tho doubtless
    inherited ones ?
That the Pauper who lives on your pittance, that the
    Laggard who leaves not his Isle,
That the Fearful who will not adventure, that the Slothful
    who moves not a mile
From his own village centre should vote in your Coun-
    cils, and speak to your shame,
While the Manhood and cream of your People are now
    but your People in name !
Stands not the boast of our Country that the waves are
    her Realm ?—why then
Should a stretch of her Kingdom make different the
    status of those who like men
Have carried her banners beyond them ?—You give to
    your Weaklings a vote,
Give one too to your Strong and your Helpers in all
    things where a slip may devote
Your Sons, thro your lack of discretion, to danger and
    risk and to wrong ;
Yea, let them have their say in the Nation who in action
    have shown themselves strong !
For the war-cloud is looming up nearer and its hail may
    fall first on their shores
Who to-day are with you in the Desert ; or on those who
    have toiled in your cause,
Your gallant Canoe-men in Egypt, whose Land may taste
    first of the fight
On their North-West unguarded Pacific, e'en now while
    this sentence I write.—

Was cause ever juster than ours is or insult endured
by the Strong
More cooly than by us who reason 'gainst hope, who
have waited so long,
Till we weary of "incidents" *trifling* that are *only* the
slaughter of Friends,
The breaking of treaties and compacts, and all that the
Muscovite sends
With addition of insult on insult for the ear of the Eastern
Bazaars.—
Perchance for the breaking of Russia, the end of the
line of the Tzars !
Let air and let freedom upon her and her Empire will
crumble, and rust
Should you sprinkle with gold the endeavour that waits
in the Nihilist' dust
To rise for the liberty coming, that often has fallen to be
free,
That is pent as the waves of a lake by dyke from the
surge of the sea ;
Once shatter the wall and the Builders will have ample
and more on their hands
Than will keep them employed on their borders and
respite the neighbouring Lands.—
It is steel that must settle the question :—let the question
be settled, and hurled
For ever away with a Russia struck out from the map of
the world ;—
Let Poland be once again Poland, Caucasia and Finland
re-rise,
To Germany give back her Peoples that Russia can not
russianise,

Bring back the old Map of the Baltic !—'Tis well :—
we're dividing the prey

Ere the prey has been torn from the talons of the fierce
Beast that stands in the way.—

Good and true !—But the Bear and the Lion, mark you,
are not, Sparrows at strife,

And he who in death-struggle closes can only come out
with his life

With his Foeman's reft life in his red hands !—If we
fight, let us fight to the end,

And grimly determined for ever to finish whatever might
lend

To the Future renewal of warfare. Perhaps it is Hellish
to fight,

But while we do wrong let us do it so wrong none can
take it for right

And act as true sons of that Kingdom.—I am not here
to argue the point

Or the rights and the reasons of Ethics, or if things are
all out of joint.—

Let us finish with frivolous chatter of peace and goodwill
and the like,

There *is* ' peace ' for the strong and the fearless ' goodwill ' for the ready to strike ;

Some day there may be a Millennium, to day but the
fittest survive,

What we want here is iron to win us the bread that will
keep us alive !—

How fearful !—Sweet Friend and objector, remember
the food that you eat

Is the outcome of slaughter. You want it.—No harm
if you butcher your meat.

The Shark and the Wolf are your Brothers! Sweet
    Friend, look things straight in the face
The Shark and the Wolf have to struggle, so have
    Nation with Nation and Race!
Our duty 's to see that we win and that England goes
    first in the strife—
Be it peaceful or fierce we've to meet it and make the
    best compact with Life.—
    Is it War! Do I love it? I hate it! I hate it so
      much, I would make
It so fearful a thing, and no pastime, that the boldest
    of Statesmen would shake
Ere they hurled against Nation a Nation, not to play till
    one side lost its breath
With the loss of some Treaty or Province, but extinction
    and National Death!—
I admire not State-craft as profession, the ribbons on
    Diplomat's coats,
The tuning to titles of measures to juggle unwary of
    votes,
And I think they do better for England and the Future
    will hold them more dear
Who have died in the front of her battle not lied in her
    Parliament here!
—In her Parliament, aye, where all England should
    speak, not a section or class—
By England I mean not this Island, but all that which
    cometh to pass
In an England of Islands, of Countries, of Continents!
    Who shall set bound
To that England I see in the future, that girdles the earth
    with the sound

Of the speech that made Shakespeare and Milton, that
    Chaucer lisped sweet at its dawn,
That burned on the lips of Sir Richard when the little
    Revenge was o'erborne,
That sharpened the pikes of the Boarders, made hands
    grip, and rang thro their cheers,
When you feel, as you read, they were Devils—aye, but
    English, the old Bucaneers !
  And here if I speak over strongly it is that my heart
    has its fires
That are hot against luke-warm Detractors that Love not
    the Land of their Sires,—
True Churchmen of Laodicea, with ever some doubting
    to preach.—
Joined with these others too, certain others, made
    manifest here by their speech,
And, held they the place of Gehazi, small doubt but that
    each one would go
From out of the presence of the Prophet, a Leper and
    whiter than snow,
With the price of his shame in his fingers ;—the race of
    the talents and fine
New changes of raiment survive and lift up the voice of
    their line,
We have them among us to-day :—some have swallowed
    the subsidy tried,
Good hap to the Ranks of the Rouble whose Penmen
    have fearlessly lied !
To think they are English !—But let us look now to some
    others that set
A new cry against us and mutter, we thank them, with
    warning regret.—

What have we with the Brokers of Berlin or the Bourse
that has bought for a rise,

They are pinched and are frothing forthwith in words
they but lamely disguise,

And if we count only from this point already we've won
in the fray

That waits but the sword-tilt of Brennus to settle the
matter for aye !—

Ah, Knaves, that would stand in our pathway, who know
not our power and our might ;

We have Knaves too in England at home but I think
none who *fear* for the fight !

And I—I am only a voice, not of Party, or Placemen,
or Bribes,

And I speak in the might of my mission, with authority
—not as the Scribes—

Nor with that of the young Politician who travels by
Steamer and Train

And studies the World from his Guide Book to retail to
his Clients again—

A Poet can see and consider, a Poet can speak for the
truth,

And look to the mind of the matter : though the foolish
may sneer at his youth,

Not many have wandered so widely, so mixed with the
dealings of men,

That the heart takes the thought of the Greybeard ere
the years to their twenty add ten—

I speak as a fool—for the most Folk that prate from
Parochial Schools

Have the brains of the Ape, and its mischief,—it is folly to
reason with Fools !

We have naught with the Vermin of Party, the Panders
    to folly and crime

Who seek but a sop from the Nation.—Ah, well, but there
    cometh a time

When the plaster will fall from the ulcer and all men will
    see it and make

The Leper depart from their presence, if only for cleanli-
    ness sake !

  But I speak for the Men of the People who are glad
    of the might of the Past,

And are full of a hope for the Future, and take up the
    Present to cast

Under the feet of the Present its sorrow and evil and
    wrong,

Who would not drag down to dead levels but raise with
    the might of the Strong.

Who thrill at the thought of an Empire whose ends are
    the ends of the Earth,

Whose powers are not Armies or Navies, but whose
    strength is the Home and the Hearth,

And the men who will die to defend them, whose work
    is the work of the whole,

Who are workmen, true workmen, my Brothers, not only
    workmen at the Poll.

Who are Democrat, Tory, Republican, call them what
    name ye may list,

But who, in the bond of their birth-right, are English,
    Imperialist !

An Empire whose greatness none dreamed of, whose
    might is the might of the Sea ;

Whose crown is the lives of her Children who have dared
    and have died to be free,

G

And who come to the daring again ; not, indeed, as the
    careless and light,
But as men who hold freedom in honor, and will strike
    for the truth in the fight.—
Look abroad, see our Brothers are ready ! O Fathers, and
    Brothers, and Sons !
O Line from the loins of old England ! O Kinsmen, out
    yonder the Guns ;—
They have flashed you defiance ! O children, flash round
    thro the Nations of Men,
That the banner of England is shaken, flung out on the
    war-wind again !

FINIS.

PRAIRIE PICTURES.

Cloth Boards, 8vo, 5s.

————:o:————

" Mr. Grant's new volume shows a union of very real and original imagination, with the metrical power of which the 'Year of Life' was a pledge. 'Permanent' is full of fancy and humour, and 'Lilith' is exquisitely expressed. But we prefer the 'Rolling Prairie' for its vigorous movement and unity of *motif.*"—*The Times.*

" 'Prairie Pictures' is the third volume of Poems which Mr. Grant has given us in three years. This is rapid writing. His first volume is so full of splendid promise, that his last, true and vigorous as it is, disappoints us. Much of the disappointment, however, is due to the subject. Mr. Grant is at his best when he treats of human thought and feeling. The 'Prairie Pictures' are landscape sketches written in compliance with the advice of a critic, which is prefixed as the *motif* of the book. They are masses of flowers and waving grass, over which the birds sing and the butterflies hover, and in whose undergrowth thousands of nimble creatures hide and dart. The first effect of this luxuriant, multitudinous life upon the mind is as bewildering as Sir Walter Scott's endless costumes and furniture. On Mr. Grant's behalf it may fairly be pleaded that the first effect of the prairie itself is bewildering, and that hence he is true to nature. Unlike the costumes and the furniture, the prairie growths improve on a second reading. They are bold, clear sketches, presented by the simplest method possible. Often no more is done than just to name the flower, and give its characteristic colours, and yet we feel that we see it. * * * There is an interesting relationship between the 'Prairie' and the 'Rolling Prairie,' at first sight two such different poems. 'The Prairie' is the scene presented to the natural eye. The 'Rolling Prairie' is the same scene reflected in the magical glass of imagination, when the winds of the spirit have blown over it, and the light of the soul has transfigured it. The first is, unfortunately, too long to quote. The second we would venture to praise were it less beautiful, less holy ;— * * * 'Lake Lands' has got the rest and the hush of the water in it. 'Pike Pools' is a fine graphic little piece. * * * On the whole, we must confess that the 'Prairie Pictures,' with one glorious exception, are too much the work of Mr. Grant's perceptive faculties rather than of his heart and imagination. Here and there

we come upon divine echoes caught fresh from the lips of the muse.
* * * 'Lilith,' a dream-poem, will be a mystery to the uninitiated
public ; but readers who have mastered 'Double Identity' in Mr.
Grant's first published volume will readily understand it.   There is
a fascination in its dreamy music.   The opening stanzas are perhaps
the loveliest, but it is hard to choose.   *   *   *   Three of the
Sonnets—'A Face Found,' 'Continuance,' and 'Beyond'—are
also true poems of great beauty.   'In Memoriam' everyone will
read with interest.   It is the story of the gallant engine-driver who
detatched his engine from his carriages and charged a goods train to
save the lives of his passengers by the sacrifice of his own.   *   *   *
We have formerly had pleasure in bearing cordial testimony to Mr.
Grant's power to see and skill to utter, and we find no reason now
to reverse our verdict.   By his wealth of language, by his truthful-
ness, by his passionate interest in the human, by his indignation
against national wrong and private selfishness, by his religiousness—
'by all these sure and burning signs'—Mr. Giant bids fair to be a
great Poet."—*The Literary World.*

" The present volume has a distinct freshness of theme which is
agreeable to the mind weary of the worn-out subjects of much
modern verse.   The Poems . . . are vigorous and graphic as poems,
as well as interesting and valuable as glimpses of things that are
strange to us.   *   *   *   There is one poem in Mr. Grant's book
which seems to us to be no less touching in its simple rugged treat-
ment than fine in its virile beauty of subject.   It is entitled,
'Done his Duty—and more !' and is the story of an engine-driver
who sees a goods train coming down upon the train he drives, and,
to save his passengers, uncouples his engine, charges and upsets the
approaching train, and loses his own life as a sacrifice to duty."—
The Academy.

" Mr. Grant . . . depicts with graphic force and truth some of
the most characteristic scenes of the great North West.   His Poems
possess a quality of freshness that is rather felt than definable ; and
his pictures are not 'dead pieces of nature,' as Addison says, but
have atmosphere and vitality.   Mr. Grant's powers of observation
are very considerable ; his style is individual, and his presentation
of things is full of originality and quaint suggestion, of which the
little poems called 'Permanent,' and 'Lilith,' are excellent ex-
amples."—*The Saturday Review.*

" 'Prairie Pictures' is decidedly good, and the descriptions of
North American scenery are quite enthralling, and make the
reader long for personal experience of the gorgeous *flora* with
which the Author shows so intimate acquaintance, as well as of
the various phases of life in the wilderness.   But it is not only
by his pictures of natural history that Mr. Grant's melodious
Poems are distinguished ; they contain deep and earnest thought

—witness a passage, at page 41, on the plurality of worlds ; the mystical piece, ‘ Lilith,’ dealing with ‘the n’er impossible she ’; and, best of all, ‘ Vicisti.’ Mr. Grant’s reputation will be en‐ hanced by his latest volumes.”—*The Graphic.*

“ It is all earnest work.”—*Vanity Fair.*

“ An elegant little volume from the pen of one of the most promising of our younger Poets. There is much brightness and vitality in these ‘ Prairie Pictures.’—*Sheffield Daily Telegraph.*

“ Mr. Grant’s proved *forte* is minute description.”—*Whitehall Review.*

“ Poetry is a drug in the market nowadays, probably because there are no Poets; but here is a charming little book quite out of the common run.”—*St. Stephen’s Review.*

“ * * * To this far-off region his ‘ Prairie Pictures ’ relate, and certainly the wonderful and beautiful scenes he describes in admirable verse are well fitted to inspire the poet, to charm the lover of nature, and to invite the emigrant in search of a new home. The remaining pieces are on miscellaneous subjects, but they are very interesting, and prove the Author to be endowed richly with the true poetic spirit. We find nothing trivial or slipshod here ; but everything is good, and we much commend the book for its originality and beauty.”—*The Queen.*

“ In these the prairies are stretched before us, musically and freshly. Bird and bee and blossom are there painted by a tender and loving hand. In all their varied aspects we have the wide reach of the sea-like waste of lands in the Far West. Mr. Grant has true poetic feeling and expression.”—*The Sunday Times.*

“ There is a warmth and fervour about them which ought to satisfy the most enthusiastic. * * * ‘ The Rolling Prairie,’ ‘ Pike Pools,’ ‘ Waterway,’ ‘ A Prairie City,’ are all pictured with poetic grace, and stamp the Author as a keen observer, and a master of the art of versification. In the same volume are contained ‘ Lilith,’ ‘ The Girl I Love,’ and eight sonnets, all of which are charmingly written, and indicate a distinct advance upon Mr. Grant’s previous efforts.”—*The Liverpool Courier.*

“ What strikes us most about Mr. Grant’s verse is the keenness of observation which it displays. The power of expression is often forcible and delicate. * * * There is much vigour and virility in these poems, and the pictures of Canadian life and scenery are especially fresh and striking.”—*Birmingham Daily Post.*

“ Mr. John Cameron Grant paints a minute picture of the land of the far North-West. He also describes the Bush with *almost scientific* accuracy. We admit the cleverness of these descriptions. * * * ‘ Lilith,’ that impossible she who is the haunting spirit of each man's innermost fancy, is not without merit."—*The West-minster Review.*

" From the sublime heights of absolute ignorance of Prairies, we condescendingly survey Mr. Grant's ' Prairie Pictures,' and pronounce them admirable. One thing, at least, we can confidently affirm respecting them—that they make us regret extremely never to have seen the beauties which he so vividly describes. ' Lilith ' is a poem hardly to be criticised. It holds the idea which many a painter, poet, sculptor, and musician has striven through life to embody, without accomplishing his object ; at least, to his own satisfaction. ' Vicisti' contains the germ of many thoughts, and its constant refrain—

' The waves go on, the waves go on'—

is no mournful dirge over that which is submerged, but a triumphant strain, evoked by a strong confidence that

' Christ is in the rising sea.'

Some of the shorter pieces have much beauty, and the whole volume seems to justify the belief that in the vast solitudes of the great lone land, the soul, which can rise at all above the mirk and mire of our overcrowded life, may stand very near to Him who is invisible, and receive impressions which will abide with it for ever."—*The Scottish Review.*

" Encouraged by the favourable reception of his previous collections of verse, Mr. Cameron Grant has been induced to publish this little volume, containing sketches of pleasant places and times spent in the great Agricultural centre of Manitoba. As becomes a true Poet, he has endeavoured to portray the wild scenery of his new home.* * * The first part of the volume is occupied by ' Prairie Pictures.' * * * marked by passages denoting great command of language and skill in depicting the characteristics of hitherto unsung lands. The following beautiful passage is taken at random. A cluster of sonnets display remarkable facility in the use of this form of verse."—*Edinburgh Courant.*

" We have the satisfaction of seeing that these ' pictures ' have been produced in answer to a request conveyed by a criticism in these columns. They are unquestionably effective, photographic, perhaps it might be said, in parts, rather than artistic ; but bright and full of colour, and enabling the reader to form conceptions of the reality, which are at least vivid. The catalogue of flowers in the ' Prairie ' is a striking piece of word-painting. It cannot be reckoned a fault that, relying for its effect upon the general impression, rather than on any particular details, it offers no suitable passages for extract. By way of contrast with this, and not without its touch of humour, is the ' Prairie City.' Among the other pictures, we may specially mention ' Pike Pools ' and ' After Dark,' the concluding stanza of which we will quote."—*The Spectator.*

"Mr. Grant aspires to be the Poet of the Prairies * * * he is to be congratulated upon the novelty of his subjects ; the praires, and the large corn lands, and the great lakes deserve to have their Poet." —*The Manchester Examiner.*

"We find much to admire and comparatively little to censure. Mr. Grant has worked out a manner of his own, and his pictures of forest and lake land are painted with a broad vigour which proclaims independent observaiion, and carries the reader buoyantly forward. Manitoba presents virgin soil to the poetical pioneer, and Mr. Grant may be congratulated on being first in the field. The workmanship of the book is remarkably and admirably free from the ordinary faults of descriptive poetry. That Mr. Grant possesses a large measure or the poetic spirit may be asserted without fear of contradiction. His volume is emphatically pleasant to read, and contains things which linger in the memory.—*Inverness Courier.*"

"From time to time the great West sends out voices that thrill us with the charm and freshness of their melody. First, we think, came Bret Harte, with his wonderful photograph of Californian life ; then Joaquin Miller ; and now in ' Prairie Pictures ' we have another with a claim worth looking at. Mr. Grant possesses less of dialect than his predecessors, nor has he that sympathy with men in their half-lawless state which is the chief charm of Bret Harte's stories. He has, however, on the other hand, a keen eye for Nature, and a touch that gives masterly descriptions in a verse, sometimes in a single line ; for example, take a verse or two from ' Pike Pools '—a poem that ought to delight the heart of all anglers and lovers of Nature. * * * We would willingly give our readers the whole of the poem, and a good many others in the volume, were space not thought of. In the ' Prairie,' ' Prairie City,' ' Lake Lands,' and, indeed, in almost every poem, we have descriptions which stamp Mr. Grant a Poet, and one of a high order. In this volume he has produced work which is so fresh of the prairie, river, and mountain, that the next work from his pen will be eagerly looked for by those who have had the pleasure of perusing the present volume."—*Dundee Advertiser.*

"That Mr. Cameron Grant has within him the spirit and faculty of a true Poet we have had occasion before now to say. In the pleasant little volume before us, his Muse leads us into what, in literal truth, may be termed a new field, inasmuch as the subjects that occupy the larger part of the space have relation to the more salient features in the scenery of the far North-West. Of these we are presented with a succession of pictures ; and very charming pictures they are. Such subjects as ' The Prairie,' ' The Rolling

Prairie,' ' A Prairie City,' ' Lake Lands,' ' Bush,' and so on, have never, so far as we know, been sung as they are sung here. Accurate observation of natural objects, vivid fancy, and musical numbers combine to bring before us, with great freshness and effect, not only the external features but the living feeling * * * The other poems, which, in addition to the longer poem ' Lilith,' include several sonnets, and one or two lyrics, are distinguished by true poetic feeling, fine taste, and finished versification."—*Aberdeen Daily Free Press.*

"In compliance with a suggestion by the *Spectator's* reviewer of his last book, Mr. Grant has been drawing ' bright pictures of a life which is strange to us, and interesting because it is strange.' The volume into which these pictures has been formed is smaller than either of its predecessors, ' Songs for the Sunny South,' and ' A Year of Life.' As a whole, its contents are not essentially different from Mr. Grants' previous writings. They display the same excellence and the same defect. They are the outcome of a lusty imagination in excitable sympathy with Nature. * * * The want of restraint thus indicated is the only defect we would attribute to Mr. Grant. When dealing with subjects worthy of his Muse he speaks with extraordinary eloquence. His book is studded with perfect gems of epigrammatic poetry. * * * It is in the art of this passage that Mr. Grant most notably excels. His phrasing of those cosmic perceptions which all of us have, is so vividly picturesque that the veriest common places of natural beauty are presented to us as novel. Some of Mr. Grant's critics have hinted that his transcendental theories have probably been annexed from the writings of others. We do not share in that suspicion. His utterances are too intensely living to be echoes ; and all that we can say about the harmony of his love poems with the philosophy of which Rossetti, Ruskin, Mallock, Myers, and Tirebuck are the most popular of modern exponents, is that his imagination has been at work among the secrets of the Infinite with a penetration keen like unto theirs."—*The Fifeshire Journal.*

A YEAR OF LIFE, THE PRICE OF THE BISHOP, AND OTHER POEMS.

Cloth Boards, *8vo*, *7s. 6d.*

——:o:——

"Mr. Grant is distinctly and undeniably a Poet ; more than this, within a certain compass he is a Poet of a high order. To compare him with the common ruck of rhymesters who now-a-days flood the world with Society ballads, lays of town life, and chronicles of blasphemous costermongers, or impossible poachers, would be absurd. He towers above them as the Author of the Epic of Hades towered above the small fry of his season. The promise, which was detected by critics in his earlier work, has been redeemed, and he occupies now the somewhat remarkable position of a Poet worth reading."—*The Madras Times.*

"To write a sustained poem in sonnet form, consisting of no less than three hundred and sixty-five stanzas, was rather a bold venture. The Author's earlier work had prepared us for graceful fancy and earnest thought, as well as for correct metrical expression, and there are no signs of deterioration in his present volume. Indeed, the Book is much above the average."—*The Graphic.*

"These Poems * * * are well worth reading. The Poem from which the volume takes its title is an ambitious *tour de force*, consisting of three hundred and sixty-five stanzas, each of which is a true sonnet. This, according to Mr. Grant, is 'such a very beautiful flowing and plastic verse that one should scorn to require more than four rhymes in the fourteen lines'; and that this metre possesses the qualities he claims for it his own example goes very far to prove. Hence we have little reason to regret that it is in this form that he has chosen to clothe his enlightened optimism, his ardent patriotism, his catholic humanity, his deep religious feeling, and enthusiastic love of Nature and of art. By way of affording our readers 'a taste' of Mr. Grant's 'quality'—a taste which we feel sure, will create an appetite for more—we detach, though not without a qualm, the following Shakespearian pearl from its appropriate setting :— Among the minor poems bound up with *A Year of Life*, the sonnet to Gustave Doré strikes us as peculiarly beautiful. Let us add that Mr. Grant's poetry is of that kind which 'grows' upon the reader; and that his present work, notwithstanding its obvious shortcomings, contains ample earnest of better things to come."—*Life.*

" Coming to the poem itself we can commend it. Exhibiting a grasp of style, being fluent and forcible." — *The Academy.*

" These Sonnets are always correctly and often finely expressed. They are full of wise and noble thoughts."—*The Westminster Review*

"In the great majority of these Sonnets there is displayed a quite unusual mastery of the Verse. There is much true poetry in this Volume—much that bears out the promise of Mr. Grant's first Book. But there is more than promise here : there is performance, although it is by no means the best that we hope yet to have from the pen of Mr. Grant."—*The Scotsman.*

"This is a volume of Poems of exceptional vigour and beauty."—*Public Opinion.*

" The Sonnets are full of poetic feeling."—*Dundee Advertiser.*

"It gives indications of genuine power."—*The Literary World.*

" Full of vigour, originality and promise. We cannot lay aside this suggestive book without a certain feeling of pity for the Author. What a strange destiny it is that impels those most distracted in emotion to depict human joys so livingly, and causes the most deeply doubtful to construct the most impregnable defence of faith ! "—*The Fifeshire Journal.*

"His selection of subjects might seem bold even for a modern Milton. He is a keen observer with a considerable power of imagination."—*The Guardian.*

" We are glad to note the fulfilling and perfecting of the poetic promise which his first volume contained. Mr. Grant has been singularly successful with the form of Sonnet he has chosen. We subjoin a really beautiful poem taken almost at random from among the Sonnets in *A Year of Life.* Mr. Grant undoubtedly possesses the true poetic spirit, and should in time make for himself a name among our Poets."—*The Inverness Courier.*

" Mr. Grant is already well known to most lovers of Poetry as a writer who can give melodious and poetic expression to description and narrative, as well as to the more subtle and transcendental forms of thought which deal with the religious and spiritual side of Nature. The present collection will do much to establish and strengthen his reputation."—*The Aberdeen Journal.*

" Striking thoughts well expressed."—*The Banffshire Journal.*

"If there is a daring exhibited in the form adopted, there is also daring in the plan. Yet we must say, that he is much more successful than we could have deemed it possible ; many parts of the poem are very fine. In the minor poems the Author has exhibited his old liking for the French ' Ballade' and his mastery of its intricate measure."—*The Stirling Journal.*

" There is a vigour in his verse, and beauty, and at times there is a commendable simplicity. There is much touching earnestness— such thoughts so put cannot fail in their moral effect; and there is throughout the Poem an evident purity of purpose that sends home with double force its thrilling verse."—*The Oracle.*

" Rare qualities of thought and expression, affording unimpeach- able grounds for congratulation. Mr. Grant gives ample evidence of very considerable poetic gifts. The Author is certainly seen to advantage in *The Price of the Bishop*, which has a distinct interest of its own, and is indeed a poem-drama of unusual merit."—*Notting- ham Daily Guardian.*

" He has an admirably mastery of the form of verse which he employs. Mr. Grant writes, as a rule, with fine facility and melody, and yet with vigour. Mr. Grant has a good deal of the poetic quality in his nature, and a large measure of poetic grace in thought and expression. The aim of the poem is so gigantic that the performance is dwarfed, and its real merits are apt to be over- looked."—*The Glasgow Herald.*

" We have simply thought and read as most men, and to that extent are able to appreciate the service our Author has rendered to thoughtful and earnest people. The Author displays that remark- able familiarity with Nature, along with a reverent spirit, which were so apparent in his former volume."—*The Elgin Courant.*

" These Sonnets are not only readable but enjoyable, the ideas as well as the diction being refined and poetic. In *The Price of the Bishop* there is considerable dramatic power, and some of the fugitive pieces, notably *Undertones*, contain the very essence of genuine poetry.—*Liverpool Daily Courier.*

" There is much crudeness in Mr. Grant's verse, but there is also much that is graceful, and much that is happily expressed, while earnest and lofty intention pervades the whole of his work."—*The Sunday Times.*

" That poetic faculty which he undoubtedly possesses."—*The Pictorial World.*

" Written throughout on the strictest Miltonic model."—*Cam- bridge Express.*

" Despite Mr. Grant's mysticism, all lovers of genuine poetry will recognise in him a true singer who is yet destined to produce works surpassing his previous efforts, alike in maturity of thought and perfection of versification."—*The Edinburgh Courant.*

"We accord Mr. Grant high praise."—*Nonconformist.*

"Mr. Grant has the accomplishment of verse in no mean degree, and his genius is eminently suited to the lyrical method. *The Price of the Bishops* is a powerful poem, and gives evidence of high poetic feeling."—*Sheffield Daily Telegraph.*

"Mr. Grant has lyrical power and wide range of expression."—*British Quarterly Review.*

"Taken altogether, we have not met for a long time with a volume of poetry written with so much heart-warmth, and in a style so effective in phrase and figure. It is a work of more than passing interest, and as such, we commend it to all lovers of genuine poetry."—*Aberdeen Daily Free Press.*